Ju
F
Su 3   Suhl, Yuri.
            The merrymaker.

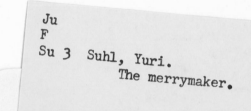

DATE	ISSUED TO
10 NOV 31	Suzanne

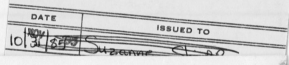

Ju
F
Su 3   Suhl, Yuri.
            The merrymaker.

Temple Israel Library
Minneapolis, Minn.

The Merrymaker

The Merrymaker

by Yuri Suhl

illustrated by Thomas di Grazia

Four Winds Press · New York

LIBRARY OF CONGRESS CATALOGING IN PUBLICATION DATA

Suhl, Yuri.
  The merrymaker.

SUMMARY: With little to eat themselves, a poor Jewish family
of eastern Europe invites a guest into their home, a merrymaker
at weddings, who eventually brings them good fortune.
  [1. Jewish way of life—Fiction] I. di Grazia, Thomas, illus.
II. Title.
PZ7.S9445Me   [Fic]   74–13182
ISBN 0–590–07346–X

PUBLISHED BY FOUR WINDS PRESS

A DIVISION OF SCHOLASTIC MAGAZINES, INC., NEW YORK, N.Y.

TEXT COPYRIGHT © 1975 BY YURI SUHL

ILLUSTRATIONS COPYRIGHT © 1975 BY THOMAS DI GRAZIA

LIBRARY OF CONGRESS CATALOG CARD NUMBER: 74–13182

1   2   3   4   5 79 78 77 76 75

The Merrymaker

I *saw the stranger standing* by the synagogue door during the evening services and wondered who would take him home for a meal and a night's lodging. If he's lucky, I thought, he'll be invited by reb Todres, the fish dealer, and he'll have both fish and meat on an ordinary Thursday. If reb Feivish, the baker, asks him home he won't starve either. Crisp, white rolls on a plain weekday. What luxury! At reb Mendel's, the timber merchant's home, he would have a feast the kind of which some Jews have only once a year on Passover. But there was little chance of reb

Mendel inviting him. He was the richest man in town and his guests were not the kind that stood by the door. They were either renowned scholars or businessmen who interrupted their homeward journey to avoid riding on the Sabbath.

There was no question about my father taking him home because we couldn't afford it. Once, when he did bring home a guest for the Sabbath my mother was very unhappy. "You shouldn't have done it," she told him afterwards. "It's embarrassing not to be able to serve a guest a regular Sabbath meal."

"But once in a while I want to perform the *mitzvah* of 'inviting a guest' as other Jews do," my father had protested.

"Other Jews provide their wives with enough to run a house with. So don't tell me about other Jews."

"You are sinning, Dvoireh. There are Jews who are worse off than we are and still they take home a guest for the Sabbath."

"But how do their wives feel, do you know that, too?"

Since then my father had not brought home anyone from the synagogue.

I kept looking at the stranger, wondering where he came from and what his occupation was. Neither his appearance nor his manner of praying offered any clues to these questions. There was nothing distinctive about his beard, which was thick and a rusty red. His muddy, wrinkled boots and frayed caftan were the commonplace attire of the poor Jew of whom we had many in our town. Like most worshippers he prayed by heart and swayed a little.

Once when our eyes met for an instant I lowered mine quickly, in embarrassment, taking refuge in the open prayer book in my hands. I was curious to see what would happen if I looked up. I did and our eyes met again. This time he set me at ease with an impish wink. A daring thing for a Jew to do in the middle of prayer. I liked him for that.

As soon as the services were over I tugged at my father's sleeve and said, "Papa, there's a stranger by the door."

My father, who had been praying with his face to the wall, turned around and studied the man. "Seems like our kind of guest," he said, to my surprise. "He won't get much to eat but on a Thursday he wouldn't expect much anyway. Go over and ask him if he would like to come home with us."

I walked up to the man and, in a trembling voice, said, "My father wants to know if you'd like to be our guest for tonight."

He took my chin in his hand, gave me a big smile
and said:

Birds to the nest,
Cows to the stable,
I'll be a guest
At your table.

I was so startled by his rhymed reply that I forgot
what he had said. "What shall I tell my father?" I asked.

Tell your father that I said
If he offered me some bread,
And a pillow for my head,
The Lord will all his prayers heed
And reward him for his deed.

I stood there, transfixed, waiting for more rhymes to
tumble from his mouth. I didn't even notice that my
father was already standing beside me.

"Sholem Aleichem," he extended his hand to the
stranger.

"Aleichem Sholem," the other replied.

"Chaim Kenner is my name," my father said, "and
this is my son, Shloimeh, my only one."

"Naftoli Boimel from Betchootch. I have three, may

[12]

they be healthy, two girls and a boy. The boy is your son's age. How old are you, Shloimeh?"

"Ten," I said.

"So I guessed it exactly."

"Do you have lodging for tonight, reb Naftoli?" my father asked.

"Not yet, reb Chaim."

"Then you are welcome to stay with us."

"I am grateful for your kindness."

"I cannot promise you a feast, but you will not go away hungry from the table, God forbid."

I wondered how my father could say this when I myself went away hungry from the table after each meal.

"In a home where one is welcome," the man said, "a piece of bread and a piece of herring is also a feast."

"That, I can assure you, you will have."

I was disappointed. The magic was gone. The stranger spoke ordinary words like everyone else. I wondered if I would hear him rhyme again. On the way home from the synagogue I walked abreast of him, my ears cocked, straining not to miss a single word. In plain, unrhymed language, reb Naftoli told my father that he was a *badchen*, a merrymaker at weddings.

[14]

No wonder he could speak in rhyme. That was a special talent that only a *badchen* possessed. I had been to several family weddings, but at none of them was there a *badchen*. And now I'll have one in my own house. What a piece of luck! Wait till the boys in *cheder* hear of this!

"Is there a *badchen* in this town, reb Chaim?" the man asked.

"In this town a *badchen*?" my father chuckled. "What would a *badchen* do in this town except die from hunger?"

"But people do get married here, reb Chaim."

"Yes, praised be the One Above. But you know how it is with weddings. The rich man wants a *badchen* with a reputation. So he'll bring one over from a big city like Cracow or Lemberg. And the poor man is lucky if he can afford a few fiddlers."

"Tell me, reb Chaim, and a *shadchen* you have in your town?"

"Matchmakers we have two," my father said.

"Two matchmakers and not a single merrymaker!"

"The two I mentioned are the professional ones. But what Jew is not a matchmaker on the side? Anyone who can't tie a proper knot on a cat's tail tries his hand at matchmaking. Not so long ago the whole town was talking about a trial involving matchmakers' fees."

"How has that come about?"

"Very simple," my father said. "Reb Gedalie, the flour merchant, married off one of his five daughters. May we both earn in a week what he spent on duck alone. After such a feast it was difficult to go back to herring and potatoes. So reb Getzel, the *shadchen*, claimed that he was responsible for the match, and reb Borech, the middleman, claimed that he also had a hand in it. Reb Borech, you must remember, is a pauper seven times over, may God not punish me for the words, and he tries to earn a groschen wherever he can. When both came to collect their fees reb Gedalie said, 'I pay only one matchmaker. And if you two have a conflict take it to the rabbi and let him straighten it out.' And so it was. Reb Getzel took reb Borech to the rabbi."

"And what was the rabbi's verdict?"

"Our rabbi, reb Duvidl, may he live long, is a true sage. King Solomon himself couldn't have come up with a more just verdict. This is what he said: 'That the children of Israel should multiply there is no question. That anyone who assists in this sacred commandment deserves to be rewarded there is also no

[16]

question. And who will question that Jews have to earn a living? So it stands to reason that reb Getzel, who is a full-time *shadchen,* should get the larger part of the fee. And reb Borech, who is only a part-time *shadchen* should get the smaller part of the fee. And let peace reign in the House of Israel.' Nu, what do you say to that?"

"A very just verdict, indeed. And how did the matchmakers take it?"

"Naturally, they wouldn't go contrary to the rabbi's decision. But since that day the two haven't spoken a word to each other. And if they happen to meet on the same sidewalk, one of them, usually reb Getzel, crosses over to the other side of the street."

*A*s soon as we entered the house my father called out, "Dvoireh, I brought home a guest for supper."

Mother, who was standing by the stove, merely turned around, as if to see whether father was joking. But when she saw the stranger her face dropped, and in a voice that was barely audible she said, "Welcome to our house."

"This is reb Naftoli," my father said, as he led the man past my mother to the living room. "He's from Betchootch."

I stayed behind in the kitchen and whispered to

Mother, "He's a *badchen*, our guest. He can rhyme. Twice already he rhymed for me in the synagogue."

"So a great fortune has struck me, he can rhyme!" my mother said, unhappily. "Let him rhyme up something to eat if he's such a rhymer. Oh, why does your father do these things? Of all days he had to pick today to bring home a guest! Chaim," she called out.

"Yes, Dvoireh."

"Be so kind and come here a minute."

My father came into the kitchen and said, "You want something, Dvoireh?"

"Yes, I want you to have a little more consideration for me. You brought home a guest. What shall I feed him, my troubles?"

"Whatever we will eat, he will eat," my father said, placatingly. "Today is Thursday, not the Sabbath. I already told him not to expect a feast."

"Did you ask me at least what *we* have to eat?"

"What's there to ask? Roast duck I know we don't have. He's a poor *badchen*. He'll be satisfied with whatever you give him."

"He will have to be satisfied with very little then. I have one herring for the three of us and a very ordinary potato soup."

"So you'll slice the herring in four, add a little water to the soup, and we'll manage."

"Thank you for the advice," she said, and began to busy herself around the stove. My father went back to the living room and I followed him.

I sat down next to the *badchen*. Mother had somehow managed to divide the herring in a way that gave each part the appearance of a sizeable portion. Garnished with an extra slice of onion and several slices of white radish it looked like a plateful. Throughout the time he was eating our guest said nothing. But when his plate was empty and the last drop of herring juice wiped up with a piece of black bread, he turned to my mother and said:

Thank you for that very tasty dish.
You can make ordinary herring
Taste like Sabbath fish.
You have many virtues I am sure,
But the greatest virtue is a heart that's pure.
May you know no want, may you only know plenty
And may you live to be a hundred and twenty.

For the first time since the stranger had come into the house my mother smiled. "Thank you for the compliment, reb Naftoli,"she said, without looking directly at him. "And may I give you one in return. Some people find it difficult to express themselves in ordinary words, but you can speak in rhyme. A blessed gift from the One Above."

I wanted to run out and call my friend, Moishele, so that he, too, could see the *badchen* and hear him rhyme, because tomorrow, right after breakfast, the merry-maker would be gone. But what if he rhymed again while I was out calling Moishele? I decided not to budge from my seat. I inched up to him as close as possible and didn't take my eyes off him. He took his beard in his hand and began to hum a melody. I had a feeling he was going to rhyme again and I was right.

> *The baker to his oven,*
> *The tailor to his shears,*
> *The* badchen *to the wedding,*
> *And the bride dissolves in tears.*
> *With the* badchen *at the wedding*
> *It is lively have no fears;*
> *The in-laws rock with laughter*
> *And the bride dissolves in tears.*

Magic! Real magic! I thought, gaping with wonderment

at the merrymaker, and right then and there I made a secret vow that I would become not a merchant, not a scholar, not even a rabbi, but a *badchen* like our guest so that I could talk in rhyme whenever I felt like doing so.

"That you're as good a *badchen* as the best of them I see," my mother said, as she dished out the soup. "But do you get any calls for weddings? A *badchen* without a wedding is like a cantor without a synagogue."

"Worse," reb Naftoli said. "A cantor, even one with a poor voice, can, at least, count on the High Holidays for a position. But a *badchen* depends entirely on chance. But if you look at it another way, the *badchen* has an advantage over the cantor. You will ask how? So I'll tell you. Real cantors there are few, but Jews who call themselves cantors there are many. They drink a few eggnogs and they think they are ready for the pulpit. But a *badchen*, if I may say so, is a bird of another kind. If he doesn't possess a real instrument, no amount of eggnogs will help him. He must be able to draw tears and laughter at will, and when the moment comes for him to stand behind the bride he must make her wail and all the wedding guests with her." He took

[24]

his beard in hand, cleared his throat and, in the familiar chant of the *badchen*, recited:

> *O, weep, bride, weep*
> *And do not tame your tears,*
> *You have come to the end of your maiden years.*
> *Until now your life was without a care,*
> *From now on new burdens you must bear,*
> *A mother to children you shall be,*
> *And to a husband a devoted wife,*
> *No longer will you like a bird be free*
> *But harnessed to the cares of life.*
> *So weep, bride, weep*
> *And do not tame your tears,*
> *You have come to the end of your maiden years.*

"True. So very true," my mother said, and began to dab her eyes with a corner of her apron.

"Look at her," my father said, "you'd think she was a bride!"

"And speaking of brides," the *badchen* said, turning to my father, "do you know of any weddings coming up in town, or of any engagements of long standing?"

My father thought for a moment then shook his

head. "Dvoireh, do you know of any?" he said to Mother.

"Come to think of it, yes," my mother said. "Only this morning, at the market, I heard that Zalmen the herring man's daughter is getting ready to marry Berke, the baker's son."

"One pauper marrying another," my father said. "Hardly a wedding for a *badchen*."

"It's not to be dismissed so lightly, reb Chaim," the *badchen* said, "a wedding is a wedding."

"A *wedding is a wedding,* that's true. And may the children of Israel continue to multiply. But what has it got to do with being able to afford a *badchen?* Zalmen, the herring man, is a pauper seven times over, God shouldn't punish me for the words."

"True, reb Chaim. Zalmen, the herring man, will not go looking for a *badchen.* But when a *badchen* goes looking for Zalmen, the herring man, that's an entirely different story. When a *badchen* appears at his doorstep on the eve of the wedding and says to him, 'Reb Zalmen, one marries off a daughter only once. I will enliven your wedding for whatever you wish to pay me,' what has he got to lose?"

"True, but what has the *badchen* got to gain?"

"May we both have so many good years as at how
many poor weddings I performed and didn't come away
empty-handed. You will ask how? So I will tell you. At
every wedding, however poor, there is at least one well-
to-do in-law, either on the bride's or on the groom's
side. If he isn't well-to-do, he is well off. And if he isn't
well off, he is better off than some of the other in-laws.
The rest is up to the *badchen*. If he is not a *shlimazel*
and knows his business, one relative can make the
wedding worth his while. And if the One Above helps
and there is one such relative on the bride's side and
one on the groom's side, it could be a very lively wedding, indeed. You will ask how? So I'll tell you. In the
first place the *badchen* must have a nose. He must be
able to smell out that rich or well-to-do relative from
among all the other wedding guests. He must find out
what his name is, and what his father's name is, where
he is from and whatever else he can find out about
him. Then, at the proper moment, the *badchen* gets up
on a chair and, in his best chant, calls out:

And now dear guests and in-laws from far and near,
What I have to say you must carefully hear.
The time has come to introduce to you
A very worthy and honorable Jew,

[28]

A man of reputation for the whole world to behold,
A man of learning with a heart of gold.
His charitable deeds are known far and wide,
He is none other than reb Flekl, the son of reb Shtekl,
An uncle of the bride.
So play, musicians, play,
Strike up a tune that is lively and gay.
The first tune you'll play I announce with pride
Is in honor of reb Flekl, the son of reb Shtekl,
An uncle of the bride.

"And when you're finished with the bride's uncle you introduce the groom's uncle. As you see, reb Chaim, there's more to a *badchen's* performance than rhyming for the bride. The bride weeps and the uncles pay. And what, if I may ask, are you doing for a living, reb Chaim?"

"I am an agent for the Atlas Life Insurance Company, a representative for the Singer Sewing Machine Company, and I do a little tutoring on the side."

"In other words," my mother added, "many trades and few blessings."

"Why should you sin, Dvoireh?" Father said. "Thank God, we are living and even manage to have a guest for supper."

Mother's only comment was a sigh. She rose, went into the kitchen and returned with four glasses of tea and several poppy seed cookies. They were leftovers from the Sabbath, which Mother had put away for some special event. Father smiled at her, pleased that she had had the foresight.

"They melt in your mouth," the *badchen* said, as he reached for his second cookie. "I don't remember when I last tasted such delicious poppy seed cookies."

"Eat them in good health," my mother said.

He did. And with each cookie he found another compliment for Mother's baking. But I was disappointed. For the herring he rhymed, the cookies he praised in ordinary language.

◍　　◍　　◍　　◍　　◍　　◍　　◍

*T*he next morning when my father came into my room, the *badchen* had gone. "Where's reb Naftoli?" he said, shaking me awake.

I looked at him through half-open eyes and mumbled, "Here, at the wedding, behind the bride."

"What wedding? What bride? What are you babbling about?"

He shook me again and this time when I looked up my mother was standing beside him. "He must have been dreaming," I heard her say.

I couldn't understand. It was so real . . . the wedding . . . the *badchen* standing behind the bride, chanting his rhymes . . . the bride weeping . . . .

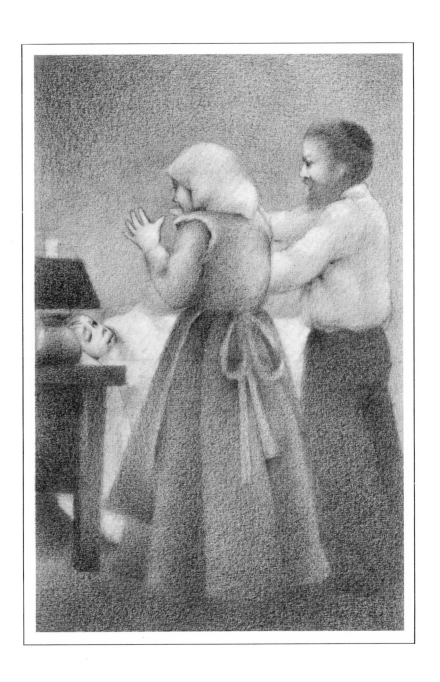

"You didn't hear him get up and leave?" Father asked.

I looked about me and was surprised to find myself in bed.

"Do you hear what I am saying, Shloimeh?"

"What?"

"You didn't hear him leave?"

"No," I said, and felt like crying. To have slept in the same bed with him and not to hear him leave! Maybe, if I had been awake, he would have made a parting rhyme for me. Now I couldn't recall a single rhyme, not from the night before and not from the dream.

"Your *badchen* left without a thank you and without a good-by," Mother said to Father. "Not nice."

"Dvoireh, you forget that today is Friday. The man wants to be home for the Sabbath with his family, and Betchootch is a long way from here. He must have left very early. I think it was considerate of him not to wake us."

"To tell the truth I'm relieved that he chose to go home for the Sabbath. The thought that he might remain here worried me all night."

"And I must say I'm a little disappointed. I wish he had remained. From a Jew who travels around you hear what's going on in the world. When can you talk leisurely if not on the Sabbath?"

"You can afford to say this because you don't have my worries. Here it is, Friday morning and I still don't have a thing for the Sabbath."

"With God's help you'll manage."

"With God's help and a little borrowing."

"So you see it worked out well all around. We fulfilled the commandment of inviting a guest and the guest left just in time. Hurry, Shloimeh, get dressed or we'll be late for the second services."

Mother left the room so that I could get out of bed. Father followed her out. When I reached for my shoes under the bed, I spotted the *badchen's* straw valise. "He's here!" I called out excitedly.

Both Mother and Father came running into the room. "Who's here?"

"The *badchen*," I said, pointing to the valise.

"You see," Father said to Mother. "And you were ready to accuse a pious Jew of leaving without a thank you."

"What does it mean, Chaim?" Mother asked, looking worried.

"It means that he got up at dawn to pray with the

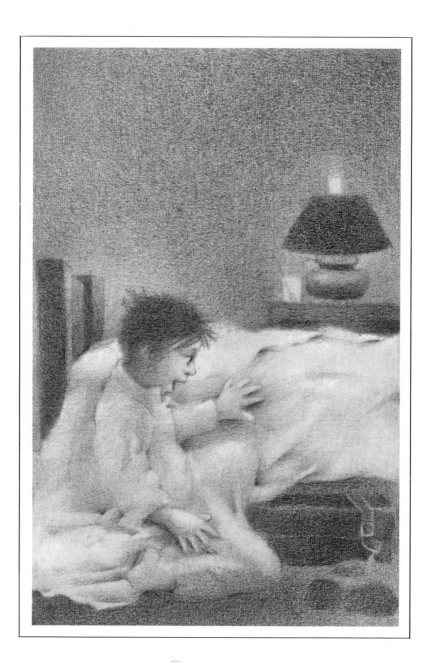

first services so that he could start out early on his long journey home. That's what it means." He raised the valise top and we all looked in. "You see, his things are here but his prayer shawl and phylacteries are missing because he took them to the synagogue."

"If that's all it means, then I better go in and boil up some coffee. He'll be here any minute. I have nothing but coffee and bread, Chaim. Not even a piece of herring."

"You'll give him whatever you have. He'll be satisfied, I'm sure."

We waited a little, and when the *badchen* didn't show up, Father and I started out for the synagogue. There we learned from the sexton that our guest had indeed prayed with the first services and had left soon thereafter. This puzzled us a little. Could it be that he had started out on his journey without his valise?

When we returned from the synagogue, Mother said, "And where's the *badchen*? I thought you'd bring him home."

"He hasn't been here yet?" Father asked.

"Not a sign of him. And something tells me, Chaim, that we're having a guest for the Sabbath."

"Don't make any hasty predictions, Dvoireh. He'll

[37]

show up any minute, take his valise and go. In the meantime give me a bite of breakfast."

Secretly I hoped that the *badchen* would remain with us for the Sabbath. I knew what worried Mother, but little as there was to eat I was ready to share it with him to hear him rhyme again.

After breakfast Mother said, "Nu, Chaim, what do I do now?"

"Do what you would ordinarily do at this time. Get ready for the Sabbath."

"Ordinarily I would be preparing now the dough for the *chaleh* and the noodles. But today, of all days, I have barely enough white flour for one. If I bake a *chaleh*, there are no noodles, and if I make noodles, there's no *chaleh*."

"Then let's forego the noodles. A Sabbath table without a *chaleh* is not a Sabbath table."

"As it is, it'll be a very small *chaleh*."

"A small *chaleh* is better than no *chaleh*."

"So it's no noodles, a small *chaleh*, and a guest for the Sabbath! My face burns with embarrassment when I think about it."

"So what do you propose we do, turn him out? When other Jews are bringing home a guest for the Sabbath,

we will tell ours to go? That we will not do," Father said, emphatically.

Mother turned her head away as though she were about to cry.

"How much flour do you need?" Father asked, "Will half a kilo do? Reb Gedalie trusted us for so much he will trust us for another half a kilo."

"I'll go for the flour," I said. "I went last time and reb Gedalie gave it to me on trust. Maybe he'll give it to me again."

"You I need for another errand," Mother said. "I need a few things from the grocery and I can't show my face there anymore. As for the flour, since I have no chicken we can do without the noodles. For ordinary beef soup, kasha and beans will suffice."

"So meat we have, thank God," Father said.

"When did we have a Sabbath without meat? It's chicken we rarely have. I'd sooner forego the fish than the meat."

"So fish we don't have either?"

"Not yet. But reb Zalmen, the herring man, who buys off the leftovers from reb Todres to sell on Friday, offers some nice bargains. The fish are no longer live but they're still fresh, and when you chop them up you don't know the difference anyway. I must run there right now or I'll miss that, too. Do you have any money?"

Father put his hand into his pocket and took out some change.

"If I give it to you, I won't have enough for the bath for Shloimeh and myself," he said.

"Never mind. Keep it," Mother said. "I don't owe reb Zalmen a groschen. He'll give it to me on trust." She picked up her shawl and draped it around her. "And if the *badchen* comes, pour him the glass of coffee I left on the stove. I must run if we're to have fish for the Sabbath."

"Fish for the Sabbath! Fish for the Sabbath!" the *badchen*'s voice came booming into the room, and presently the *badchen* himself appeared in the doorway loaded down with bundles.

"We have been wondering where you were, reb Naftoli," Father said.

"I was out on business, seeing the in-laws," the *badchen* replied matter-of-factly. "Right now I'm coming from reb Zalmen's store. The herring man, you know." He walked over to the table and put the bundles down. The first bundle he unwrapped contained

two big fish and several small ones. "That's all he had left," he said, somewhat apologetically.

"Why, reb Naftoli," Mother said, "you have enough fish here not only for the Sabbath but for a whole week afterwards."

"And this," said the *badchen*, unwrapping a smaller bundle, "he threw in for good measure—a few herrings."

"And what's in here?" I blurted out, pointing to a big paper bag.

"This is from Berke, the baker's son," the *badchen* said, pulling a large *chaleh* out of the bag. "He gave me a choice between flour and a ready-baked *chaleh*, so I took the *chaleh*. However, Mrs. Kenner, if you prefer to bake your own, I'll take flour next week."

"Next week?" Mother said.

"Yes. The wedding was set for three weeks from this Sabbath. This means that for the next three weeks we will not lack in herring, fish and *chaleh*, thanks to you."

"Why thanks to me, reb Naftoli?"

"Because you told me that the herring man and the baker were about to become in-laws. With such information I can go a long way."

[43]

"How about a bite of breakfast, reb Naftoli, you must be starved."

"No, thanks. I've already had two breakfasts, one with each in-law. What I will do right now is take a walk around town and find out who else is planning a wedding. As it is written in the holy books: Let the children of Israel multiply.

> *And I, Naftoli* badchen, *cannot afford to sleep.*
> *For if you do not sow you do not reap.*
> *My job is to make the guests gay,*
> *The in-laws pay,*
> *And the brides weep.*

When he had gone, Mother took off her shawl and said, "I had better get busy right now if I'm to cook all that fish. And I think I'll make noodles also. Even in a meat soup a few noodles add a Sabbath flavor."

"You see," Father said, triumphantly, "I told you with God's help you'd manage."

Temple Israel

Minneapolis, Minnesota

In Honor of the Bar Mitzvah of

J. PHILLIP DWORSKY

By his parents,
Mr. and Mrs. Mischa Dworsky
April 29, 1978